The Story Puppy

Other titles by Holly Webb

The Story Puppy

Holly Webb
Illustrated by Sophy Williams

For Hattie

STRIPES PUBLISHING LIMITED
An imprint of the Little Tiger Group
1 Coda Studios, 189 Munster Road, London SW6 6AW

A paperback original
First published in Great Britain in 2020

Text copyright © Holly Webb, 2020
Illustrations copyright © Sophy Williams, 2020
Author photograph © Charlotte Knee Photography

ISBN: 978-1-78895-220-0

MIX
Paper from
responsible sources
FSC® C020471

The Forest Stewardship Council® (FSC®) is a global, not-for-profit
organization dedicated to the promotion of responsible forest management
worldwide. FSC defines standards based on agreed principles for
responsible forest stewardship that are supported by environmental, social,
and economic stakeholders. To learn more, visit www.fsc.org

10 9 8 7 6 5 4 3 2 1

Chapter One

Jack stared down at the page in front of him. The words seemed to be getting all blurry round the edges and he blinked hard. He was not going to cry. He was not.

It wouldn't have been quite so bad if it were Mr Gardner, their teacher, that he was trying to read with. But it was Amarah's mum.

Jack had been really pleased when Amarah told him her mum was coming to help out with hearing their class read. He liked Amarah's mum – he'd known her for years, ever since Amarah's family had moved in next door.

It was different now that Amarah's mum was trying to get him to read out loud, though. Every time he saw her over the fence, he was going to remember sitting here. He'd been fighting to read this sentence for what felt like hours.

"Try and sound it out," Amarah's mum said gently.

"I can't," Jack muttered.

"I bet you can if you try."

"No, I can't!" Jack banged the book down on the table. Stupid book! He'd thought it would be good, when he picked it. He loved dogs and the book had a photo of a glossy golden retriever on the front. The dog's dark eyes looked right at him and its tongue was hanging out, as though it had just been for a run.

It shouldn't be so hard – all Jack wanted to do was read about the dog. But the words just kept swimming away.

"Maybe we should take a break?"
Mrs Iqbal suggested. "You've worked
really hard today, Jack."

Jack didn't say anything. He fixed his
eyes on the edge of the table, hoping
the bell was going to ring. Waiting
for Mr Gardner to say it was someone
else's turn to read. What made it worse
was that he *had* worked really hard –
he'd been trying and trying. But it
was no good. The words just didn't
make sense.

Mrs Iqbal glanced round. "Oh
– there's Elsa. It's her turn to read
next."

Jack was almost sure she was glad to
get rid of him.

Jack slouched back down the corridor to his classroom. The rest of the class were doing maths and he was good at maths. Numbers did what they ought to, not like letters. But he was still feeling miserable, and antsy, and cross. He didn't want to sit down and work out fractions. Mr Gardner would notice if he didn't get back soon, though, and their head teacher, Mrs Bellamy, had a spooky habit of turning up whenever anyone wasn't in the right place.

Glumly, Jack opened the door to the Year Five classroom.

Mr Gardner waved at him and said, "Amarah, can you show Jack where we're up to on the worksheet, please?"

Amarah nodded importantly and as Jack slumped into the chair beside her, she started to point out the questions they'd been doing.

"All right," he muttered, grabbing a pencil.

"What's up with you?" Amarah asked, peering at him curiously.

"Nothing."

"Was it the reading?" Amarah sounded sympathetic and Jack knew she was trying to be nice, but that didn't help. It wasn't fair! Why was it so much harder for him than for anybody else? And what if Amarah's mum told her that he hadn't been able to read? Then Amarah would think he was stupid. Jack's eyes started to sting again and just in that minute he felt so angry with Amarah. And her mum.

"My reading's fine," he snapped. "Leave me alone!"

"Don't be mean!" One of Amarah's other friends, Lily, pointed her pencil at him. "Amarah's only trying to be nice."

Jack glared at her. "Just keep out of it, Lily. And stop waving that at me," he added, smacking the pencil out of her hand.

He had only meant to stop her from waggling the pencil about – he thought it would just land on the table. Instead, it sailed across the room and hit Mr Gardner's trousers.

"Now look what you've done!" said Lily. She sounded half horrified and half excited. "You're going to get in trouble."

"Oh no…" Amarah whispered, watching nervously as Mr Gardner came over to their table.

"Since you all look guilty, I'm guessing this came from one of you?" Mr Gardner said, sighing.

"Sorry, Mr Gardner," Jack muttered, staring at the table. "It was an accident."

"No, it wasn't," Lily put in and

Amarah elbowed her.

"Be more careful, Jack. I'm watching this table." Mr Gardner stood there for a moment longer, as though he wanted to say something else, but then the bell rang for lunch.

"What did you do that for?" Amarah whispered to Jack as she came to stand behind him in the line for lunch.

"Leave me alone!" Jack hissed back. And then when Amarah looked like she was going to keep on talking, he darted out of his place and went further down the line to stand with Mason and James instead.

But all through lunch he could feel Amarah watching him. She was sitting with Lily, like she usually did, but she kept glancing over at him and she looked miserable. Really miserable and confused, as if she didn't know what she'd done wrong.

Jack didn't eat very much lunch.

The puppy flinched anxiously back among the weeds as another car roared past. She didn't understand what was happening. Were her people coming back? She'd tried to run after them when their car pulled away, but it was going much too fast and she was limping. She'd landed badly when they'd pushed her out of the car door – she hadn't expected it and she'd banged hard against the tarmac.

She lifted up her paw now and licked at it, whining softly. She knew the way the car had gone but she wasn't sure she could walk much further, not with her leg like this. She'd have to wait for them to come back.

She hoped it would be soon. She was so hungry and it felt like ages since she'd had anything to eat. The people had taken her mother away the day before, so she couldn't have milk and they hadn't given her any dry food that morning either.

The puppy had howled half the night with misery and she still didn't know where her mother was. She was hungry and lonely and frightened, and she didn't know what to do.

She huddled back again as the next car approached, but this time the car slowed down as it passed her. It slowed down even more, and then stopped.

The puppy wagged her tail uncertainly. Had her people come back? Perhaps her mother was in the car! She wagged a little harder and tried to sniff the air. She knew her mother's smell, but the scent was all mixed up with the dusty road and the sharp whiff of cars...

"Hey, sweetie … are you lost?"
Someone climbed out of the car and
began to walk towards her. The puppy
looked uncertainly up and down the
road. This was a stranger, she was
almost sure. Should she try to run? But
her paw… She whimpered and the
man approaching her slowed down and
began to talk again, his voice very soft.

"It's OK. Did you run off, little
thing? You're ever so skinny… Don't
be scared…" He crouched down a

little way in front of her and held out his hand. "Where's home then?" he murmured. "Come on, puppy, it's OK… Come and see me…"

The gentle voice burbled on and the puppy wagged her tail again. She didn't know him, but he was slow and quiet and he sounded kind. He might even have food and she was so, so hungry.

Hopping on three paws, the puppy struggled over to the edge of the road and sniffed his outstretched fingers. When the man picked her up and snuggled her against his jacket, she just sighed and nuzzled in. He was warm and he smelled gentle, and she didn't know what else to do.

Chapter Two

Jack was in the garden, curled up at the top of the battered old slide, when he heard the back door bang.

"Are you up there?" his sister called. "Mum says do you want a banana?"

"Hate bananas," Jack growled. He didn't actually, but at the moment he didn't feel like saying yes to anything. He'd got into trouble for accidentally on purpose kicking Mason's football too hard against a window at lunch break, and he'd kept on feeling grim and angry all afternoon.

"OK." There was a creaking sound and Mattie pulled herself the wrong way up the slide and came to sit next to him. It was a tight fit with two, but Jack was glad she hadn't gone away. Mattie didn't say anything, just closed her eyes and sat leaning back against the wooden slats.

"Are you OK?" Jack asked. She looked really tired.

"Got an essay to write." Mattie sighed. She was at college doing her A levels and it seemed like a lot of work to Jack. Mattie was always stressing about essays, and she had to fit them in round weekend shifts at the supermarket and helping out at the animal shelter down the road. "I'm putting it off, but I've got to get it started before I go to the shelter. How about you?"

Jack didn't say anything. He hadn't told Mum about his awful day, though he thought she'd probably guessed something was wrong by the way he'd marched out of school glowering at everyone. Then he sighed. Mattie was easy to talk to. She didn't look worried like Mum, or start trying to think of loads of ways to help. Mum was only being nice when she did that, but sometimes it made Jack feel worse.

"School was..." He stopped, trying to think how to put it.

"Not good?"

"Bad," he admitted, staring at his hands. "You know Amarah's mum helps out sometimes?" He waved at Amarah's garden over the fence – it was beautiful, full of roses.

"Mmm. With the reading?"

"Yeah. She was listening to me read – except I couldn't." Jack glanced sideways at Mattie. "The book was really difficult," he whispered. His voice was hoarse, as if he were about to cry. It was so hard saying it. "Difficult for me, I mean. Probably anyone else in my class could have read it."

Mattie slipped an arm round his shoulders. "I bet there are people in your class who aren't good at other things. You're really good at maths."

"Even in maths you have to read the questions," Jack muttered.

Mattie sighed. "I suppose so."

"It was horrible. I felt stupid and I didn't know what to say. Amarah's mum was really nice about it, but I bet she thinks I'm useless now. And what if she says something to Amarah?" Jack's voice shook.

"I don't think she'd do that," Mattie said comfortingly. "Look, can I read with you sometimes? Mr Gardner said it was partly just practice you needed. When he had that meeting with Mum about you getting help with your reading."

Jack leaned against her shoulder, feeling grateful. "That would be good," he agreed.

"OK. Do you feel like doing it now?" Mattie peered sideways at him, a bit doubtfully. "Or maybe when you're feeling better? We could do it before bedtime when I get back from the shelter?"

"Yeah…" Jack nodded. He could see that Mattie wanted to help, but when was she going to find the time? She was so busy with her college work and her job. And whenever she had a spare moment she went to the animal shelter to help walk the dogs or sit and stroke the cats. She'd told Jack that sometimes they needed reminding that people were nice. It seemed sad the cats had to be shown that, but Jack had visited the shelter with Mattie and he'd seen how hard the staff worked. They didn't have time to give the dogs and cats all the fuss and love they needed.

Maybe he should ask Mum to help him with reading instead, Jack thought as Mattie shot down the slide and went inside to get on with her homework. Mum always offered, but usually Jack did everything he could to get out of it – saying he was tired, or he had maths homework to do, or it was sunny so could he go outside and play with Amarah? He hated it when he got words wrong and Mum looked so worried. It made the words even harder to understand.

The puppy was hiding. This pen was more comfortable than the one she'd been kept in before – there was a soft bed and a clean water bowl and more food than she'd ever had. But it was different and it smelled strange. It was noisy too – there were so many other dogs here, all barking and howling and whining. Every time she settled down in the cosy bed, someone would start to bark and she'd leap up shivering.

The puppy had nudged her bed towards the back of the pen, squashing it up against the corner. It was big enough that if she hopped over the top and curled up tight, no one could see her – or she hoped they couldn't. The hard floor wasn't that comfortable, but she felt better tucked away.

The man who'd picked her up by the side of the road had brought her here. She'd huddled up on the car seat next to him, wrapped in his coat but still shivering. The car had growled and shuddered and she'd hated it. What if he stopped and threw her out of the door, just as her people had? When the car's engine finally died away and he reached over to pick her up, she'd cowered away from him with a whine.

The man had carried her into this place, murmuring to her gently, but then he'd left her. He went away and strangers had bandaged up her leg. It had hurt. They'd fed her and stroked her and fussed over her, but she didn't understand what was happening. Were her people going to come back? Where was her mother? Why were all these other dogs here?

The puppy whimpered and wriggled her nose underneath the padded dog bed. It was dark there and warm. She wriggled in further and she could almost not hear the barking.

Amarah grabbed the sleeve of Jack's sweater and pulled him ahead. Jack's mum was walking them all to school, but she was busy talking to Amarah's little sister Anika.

"What was wrong with you yesterday?" Amarah demanded, once they'd got far enough in front. "Why were you being so horrible?"

"I wasn't!" Jack protested, but he knew she was right.

"I had art club after school or I'd have talked to you then. You can't just pretend nothing happened. You were lucky Mr Gardner didn't send you out of the class."

Jack looked down at the pavement. "I know," he muttered eventually. "Thanks for trying to stop Lily telling."

"You did hit her pencil across the room. You can't blame her."

30

Jack only nodded and Amarah rolled
her eyes at him. "So what made you
so cross? It wasn't just Lily. You were
angry before she said anything."

Jack's shoulders drooped and he
kicked the pavement with his toe. "It
was your mum," he whispered at last.
"Don't get upset!" he added quickly. "It
wasn't her fault. She didn't do anything
bad – she was hearing me read."

Amarah looked at him for a
moment. Then she said, "I thought you
liked my mum!" in a hurt voice.

"I do!" Jack said, almost in a wail.
"But I couldn't read the book and she
must have thought I was stupid. I was
worried she would tell you."

"Oh…" Amarah looked thoughtful.
"Well, she didn't. She said she'd had

you for reading, but the only thing she told me about yesterday was that one of the girls in Year Two nearly threw up on her shoes."

"What?" Jack gasped.

"Uh-huh. Mum got her feet out of the way just in time. But when I asked who it was, she said it wouldn't be fair to tell me. She wouldn't say mean things about you either, even if she thought them. And I bet she didn't." Amarah frowned, wrinkling her nose. "Actually, I've just remembered, she said she thought you'd had your hair cut and it looked nice."

"Oh…" Jack blinked. He'd been almost positive that Amarah's mum would tell her how terrible his reading was. He'd seen them talking about it

so clearly in his head. It took him a
little while to realize he'd imagined the
whole story.

Amarah nodded. Then she added,
"What was wrong with the reading?"

Jack shrugged, but then he muttered,
"Don't know. I just can't do it."

"Was Mum any help?"

"Ummm. Not really. Sorry." Jack
glanced up at her anxiously. He really
didn't want to upset Amarah again, but
she just looked thoughtful.

"So … what are you going to do?"

"Practise with Mum. Mattie said
she'd help too, but I don't think she'll
have time with all her school stuff
and going to the shelter. And work.
She's never in. I was nearly asleep
by the time she got back last night."

Jack sighed. "What else can I do?"

"I don't know." Amarah shook her head. "I'll think about it, though. There must be something."

"Maybe." But Jack looked doubtful.

Chapter Three

Mattie slumped down on the sofa next to Jack. "Want to do some reading now?" she asked, smothering a yawn. "I've got time."

Jack felt himself tensing up, but he nodded. "I'll get the book." He was still trying to work his way through the one with the golden retriever on the cover, but he wasn't enjoying it much. It was too hard to get into the story and he kept forgetting what had happened. He had read with Mattie and Mum a couple of times over the weekend, and he thought it might be helping, but it was all so difficult.

He and Mattie struggled through a page to the end of the chapter and looked at each other hopefully. "We could stop there?" Jack suggested and Mattie nodded.

"Mum's making dinner. It'll be ready in a minute."

"Did you go to the shelter after college today?" Jack asked.

"Uh-huh."

"What's the matter?" Now that he looked at her properly, Mattie seemed really upset – Jack hadn't even noticed. His big sister tried not to tell him about the sad bits of working at the shelter, but he knew she came home worrying about the cats and dogs a lot. Mattie rested her chin on her hands and heaved a sigh. "It's one of the new dogs," she explained. Then she looked round at him. "You're sure you want me to tell you?"

"Yes…" Jack said, a little doubtfully.

"She's a puppy. Really little and

so sweet. She's white and a bit fluffy – she's probably got some Maltese in her, Lucy thinks." Lucy was the manager at the shelter. "I named her." Mattie smiled, but then her smile faded. "She's called Daisy."

"Why are you sad, if she's so sweet?" Jack asked, hugging himself tightly. He almost wished he hadn't let Mattie start telling him.

"Lucy says she's not sure we'll ever be able to rehome her."

"Why? What's the matter with her?" Jack frowned. Mattie was always telling him how the shelter staff were desperate to find good homes for all the animals. She really wanted them to adopt a dog, but Mum wasn't sure, with everyone in the family so busy with work and school. She didn't think they'd be able to look after a dog very well. Jack thought they'd be fine – every time he went to the shelter with Mattie he fell in love with a different dog, but they hadn't managed to persuade Mum yet.

"She's so nervous and miserable," Mattie explained. "She won't go to anyone and she hides whenever we bring her food or we come to clean out her pen. She doesn't trust people and she seems to hate being touched. I suppose someone was horrible to her. We get nervous dogs all the time – and dogs that are upset because their owners have died – and they hate being in the shelter. But usually they start to get a bit friendlier after a while. That's not happening with Daisy. She's been at the shelter a week and she still won't let any of us come near her. She's such a little dog – only a baby! It's not fair!"

"Oh…" Jack leaned against Mattie's shoulder. "That's really sad."

"I wish I could help her," Mattie murmured. "But I just don't know how."

Mattie was picking Jack up from school the next day – Amarah had art club and Mum was working – so she took him with her to the shelter. Jack helped out, filling up food bowls in the kitchen, and then he went for a wander around. He knew all the staff and most of the volunteers by now and no one minded him being there as long as he didn't upset any of the animals.

He tried to make a fuss of a couple of cats, but they were dozing and only peered sleepily at him when he crouched down outside their pens. There was a whole litter of black and white kittens, though, who were more interesting. Jack watched them for a while, laughing as they stalked each other's tails across the pen and then collapsed and fell asleep in a furry bundle on the floor.

After that, he went to visit the dogs. He'd seen most of them before. There were a couple of elderly dogs that nobody seemed to want to adopt – they'd been at the shelter for months. Jack's favourite was a wheezy, fawn-coloured pug. No one had been

feeling very imaginative the day he
was brought in, so he was just called
Pug. He met Jack with excited squeaky
barks and Jack sat down on the floor
by his pen and stroked him through
the wire.

Pug stood
there with
his eyes
closed and
his curled
tail whirring
while Jack
scratched
his ears and
under his
chin.

"Five more minutes, OK?" Mattie
said, hurrying past. "Just got to help

Lucy finish feeding everybody."

"OK," said Jack, then he had a thought. "Hey, Mattie!"

She turned round, walking backwards with her arms full of food bowls. "What?"

"Which pen is the new puppy in?"

Mattie stopped. "Daisy?"

Jack nodded. "I just wanted to see her…" he murmured. He hadn't been able to stop thinking about the little white puppy, since Mattie had told him how unhappy she was.

"She's not any better, Jack. Lucy told me. You'll just be upset seeing her."

"I don't care," Jack said stubbornly. "If you didn't want me knowing about her, why did you tell me?"

Mattie sighed. "I shouldn't have done.

OK… She's in the pen at the end. It's the quietest one. She doesn't seem to like the other dogs barking. I'm about to go and put her food bowl in, actually. You can come with me. Just … just don't scare her, all right?"

"Of course I won't!" Jack said indignantly. But then he nodded. "I promise I won't, Mattie. I only want to see her."

"You'll be lucky if you do," Mattie said over her shoulder as she went on down the passage. "When I went past earlier, she was hiding underneath her bed."

Jack made one last fuss of Pug and then got up to follow her. All the dogs knew it was time for their dinner and they were watching excitedly as Mattie came along with the bowls. She slipped into the pens, talking lovingly to each of the dogs as she gave them their food. Mostly they tried to eat it before she had even put the bowl down. But when they got to the pen at the end, as far as Jack could see, it was empty. Then he remembered what Mattie had said about the puppy being under her bed. It did look a bit lumpy in the middle. Was there really a puppy there, too scared to come out?

Mattie quietly opened the pen and put down the bowl. Then she came out again, looking worried. "We'll wait here for a bit," she said to Jack, beckoning him to come a little further down the passage, where they could just about see Daisy's pen. "I want to make sure she's OK. And check she's actually eating her dinner."

Jack nodded and they both stood there, craning their necks sideways. After a minute or two, the dog bed shifted a little and a whiskery white face appeared. Daisy looked around cautiously for a moment or two and then pattered across the pen to her bowl. But she kept darting anxious glances at the passage, as if she thought something scary was about to happen.

"She's so small!" Jack breathed in Mattie's ear.

"I know. She's probably about eight weeks. That's only just old enough to leave her mum. Isn't she sweet? She'd be adopted straightaway if she wasn't so timid."

Jack's stomach seemed to turn over inside him. Mattie had said that the puppy had been dumped by the side of the road. He couldn't imagine who would do that to such a tiny dog. Looking at her now, shivering as she tried to eat, he decided he'd do anything, anything to make her better.

Daisy was almost sure that someone was watching her eat. She could smell people – or thought she could. The smells here were all so strange and strong. The sharp scent of the spray the staff used to clean the pens seemed to sting her nose.

Whoever it was didn't come any

closer, though, so she kept bolting down the food. The faster she ate, the faster she could hide herself away again. She didn't want anyone to notice her. It was safe there, tucked under her bed in the warm and the dark. It reminded her of being snuggled up with her mother. And even though the hard floor of the pen made her bruised paw hurt, it was definitely better being under the bed than in it.

She licked quickly round the bowl and darted away, burrowing back underneath the squashy bed. Then she lay there, listening, tense all over, until she heard the footsteps going away.

Chapter Four

Jack had only seen Daisy for a couple of minutes, but he couldn't stop thinking about her. She was tiny, and white all over, with soft ears and a stubby, scruffy little tail. Mattie said that breakfast and dinner were the only times they really saw her – two minutes of desperate gobbling, before she scurried back to hide under her bed.

"Lucy and Adrian have both spent as much time with her as they can," she'd explained to Jack. Adrian was the other full-time member of staff at the shelter. "Lucy goes in and just sits in the pen for ages. She's hoping that Daisy will get used to her being there and come out. Though she hasn't so far. But they're so busy – the shelter's full again. Any time they spend coaxing Daisy to be friendly is time they have to take away from the other dogs and cats."

It didn't seem fair to Jack that Daisy needed help and everyone was too busy to give it to her. He wished *he* could help. But he wasn't old enough to be an official volunteer at the shelter. He didn't know anything about helping a dog like Daisy either. He'd probably get it all wrong. But he definitely wanted to see her again – even if all he saw was a little hump under her bed.

So the next day, instead of going home with Amarah and her mum and Anika, he persuaded Mattie to come and pick him up. He told Amarah why on the way to school that morning – he didn't want her to think he was abandoning her. Once he had told her about Daisy, though, she was all for it.

"Can you take a picture of her?" she asked. "Mattie could take one on her phone, couldn't she?"

"Maybe while she's eating," Jack said. "Otherwise it'll be a photo of a dog bed."

"That's so sad. I wish I could come with you. I want to go to the shelter anyway. Maybe we could persuade my mum and dad to get a cat."

"I could ask Mattie to take you with us one day?" Jack suggested.

Amarah nodded. Then she looked at Jack, chewing her lip as though she wasn't sure what to say. "Did you finish that book?"

"Almost…" Jack muttered. Mr Gardner had checked on their reading diaries the day before, and he'd done his *I'm very disappointed* face when he realized Jack was still in the middle of the book about the golden retriever.

"Mr Gardner said to do it last night!"

"Yeah, but I was at the shelter with Mattie." Jack shrugged. "I bet he didn't think I would anyway. He knows I'm useless at reading."

Amarah eyed him doubtfully. "He sounded like he meant it to me. I hope you don't get told off again."

Jack looked worried for a moment and then he grinned at Amarah. "I won't. We've got that history day, remember? There are people coming in to do a workshop. I'll finish the reading tonight. No problem."

"You'd better," Amarah said seriously. "I like our table the way it is – if you keep getting in trouble we'll all be moved round again and I'll end up sitting next to Lola or somebody else mean."

"All right, I will, I promise!" Jack sighed. "You're worse than Mr Gardner."

"Do you want to help with getting the food ready again?" Mattie suggested.

"Definitely." Jack nodded. The more he did to help out, the more time Mattie and the others would have to spend with the animals. It was called socializing. Jack hadn't really got it when Mattie had explained it to him before, but now he saw how much love and attention Daisy needed.

He measured out the food for Mattie while she ferried the bowls to the pens. They'd finished getting all the dogs' dinners ready when Mattie suddenly stopped, frowning at him. "Hang on. I've just remembered. Haven't you got homework to do? Amarah said I had to make sure you finished your book."

"I can do it later!" Jack protested.

"Uh-uh. We'll get home, you'll have dinner, you'll be really tired – you won't have time to finish it. Just go and sit in the visitors' room now."

Jack glared at her, but then he gave a massive huffy sigh and went to get his backpack. Mattie was right, though. And so was Amarah – he didn't want Mr Gardner moving them around in class either.

He was searching through his backpack for the reading book when it struck him – he had to do the reading, but it didn't matter *where* he did it. Mattie had said that Lucy went and sat in Daisy's pen to try and get her used to people. He couldn't do that – Lucy would definitely say no, in case Daisy got really scared and nipped him – but he could sit just outside her pen, couldn't he? That would be almost as good. He could sit still and not scare her, and even though he had to sound out a lot of the words he could do it quietly.

Jack hurried down the passage to the pen at the end and sat down, leaning against the wall. The floor was a bit hard, but it wasn't too bad. Besides, Daisy was lying on that hard floor all day.

"Hey, Daisy," he whispered. He could just about see the end of her tail sticking out from under the dog bed. "Are you OK? I've got to finish this reading homework, so I thought I'd do it with you." He looked at the bump under the bed for a moment – almost as though he thought she might answer him. Then he shook his head and opened up the book, flicking through the pages to the right place. He was a *long* way from the end.

"OK. So. Page forty-six. 'Benny … pushed the gate shut with his nose…'" Jack read on, slowly sounding out the hardest words.

He wasn't sure if Mr Gardner would think reading to a dog counted as reading with an adult – especially since Daisy was only a puppy and she wasn't actually listening – but Jack liked it more than reading to Mum or Mattie. He knew Daisy was there, so it still felt like he was reading to someone, but she didn't mind if he got the words wrong or took ages to work them out.

Mattie fidgeted when he read to her. He was pretty sure she didn't know she was doing it, but she always fiddled with the hem of her sweater or jiggled her feet around like she was bored. Mum sat still, but she tried to help too much. She was always telling him not to worry, when he wasn't – *she* was the one who was worrying.

He got to the end of the page and stopped for a rest, stretching out his shoulders. He'd been hunching forward, peering at the book. Then he froze. There had been a flash of white inside the pen. He was sure of it.

Had Daisy moved?

There was no sign of her now – except for that little wisp of white tail sticking out.

Slowly, Jack started to read again. He kept his face down towards the book, but every so often he rolled his eyes sideways to look into the pen. He was about halfway down the next page – and how had that happened? It felt like the fastest he'd ever managed to read anything – when a black nose appeared from

under the dog bed and the stub of
tail disappeared. Daisy was wriggling
forward. She was listening!

Jack went on. He wasn't sure he'd
be able to tell Mr Gardner what
happened on any of those pages, he
was too busy keeping an eye on Daisy,
but he *was* reading. And he liked that
he was reading about a dog to a dog.

After a few more sentences, the rest
of Daisy's muzzle edged out
from under the bed
and he could
just see her
dark eyes
glinting at
him from
under the
fabric.

"Oh…" he murmured a couple of minutes later. "Only one more chapter to go. Do you like this story?" He peered at Daisy again and went on talking quietly. There was more of her sticking out now. He could see her collar, and her front paws were showing too, one on each side of her nose. Jack flicked the pages over. The last chapter was short, only a couple of pages. He could do that. Definitely.

By the time he'd got to the very end of the book, Daisy was still lying on the floor, but only half of her was under her bed. She lay watching Jack with her nose on her crossed front paws and she really seemed to be listening. As if she was actually enjoying listening to him read. Jack couldn't remember the last time that had happened.

Chapter Five

Daisy could hear someone talking outside her pen. It was a quiet voice, speaking rather slowly. Some of the people here had tried to talk to her before – they'd sat in her pen and tried to coax her to come out and see them. She never did. She came out for food and ate it as fast as she could, but that was all. Once the lights were off and the staff had left, she crept out and snuggled on top of her bed. But at the slightest noise – another dog barking or even just shifting in its sleep – she would be straight back underneath.

Whoever was talking now hadn't tried to come in to her space. She liked that. They stopped every now and then, the sounds stumbling out. It made the noise seem gentle and she liked that too. It was hard to hear, though, underneath her bed.

Very slowly, she edged forward so that her nose stuck out. The boy's reading was clearer now, but then he stopped talking and she whisked back to the safe darkness under the bed. Slowly, quietly, he started again and Daisy wriggled out, centimetre by centimetre.

Apart from the quiet, halting voice, the dog section of the shelter was almost silent. No one was barking. Daisy let her ears flop down and she rested her muzzle gently on her paws. The fear that had been building up inside her for days eased, just a little, and her eyes half closed as Jack went on.

Jack didn't tell Mattie what had happened – he still wasn't sure he believed it anyway. It could just have been a coincidence that Daisy happened to decide to come out of her hiding place just then. But he really, really hoped not. If it was actually him helping, he had to go there again. Mattie wasn't going to be at the shelter for the next couple of days – she had shifts at the supermarket – but she always fitted in helping at the weekend. And he was going to go with her.

"Are you sure?" Mattie eyed him sleepily at breakfast on Saturday morning. "You know I'm going now

– before I have to go to work? As in, you'd better be dressed in three minutes if you really want to come?"

Jack didn't need to think about it. He dashed upstairs and threw on some clothes. He was back in the kitchen before Mattie had got halfway through her cereal.

"Is that OK, Mattie?" Mum asked, stirring her tea. "Jack won't be in your way?"

"I'm helpful!" Jack pointed out, feeling annoyed. "I put the food out for the dogs, and on Wednesday…" He trailed off. He'd forgotten he wasn't going to tell anyone about Daisy.

"On Wednesday what?" Mum asked.

"On Wednesday I did my homework at the shelter and I finished my reading book," Jack went on hurriedly.

"Oh, Jack, that's brilliant!" His mum shook her head. "Why didn't you say?"

"I've got another one." Jack sighed. "It's a non-fiction book about sharks. But it looks OK, I suppose."

He stuck the book in the pocket of his anorak when he set off with Mattie. He wanted to see if Daisy would listen to him reading again. If she came out from under the basket today, it would be like a scientific experiment, where you did the same thing again to make sure you got the same results twice.

He'd been a bit worried there would be lots of visitors looking at the dogs because it was a weekend – he didn't want a load of strangers hearing him reading. But when he asked, Mattie explained that they tried to encourage people to look at the dogs online first.

"It's upsetting for the dogs sometimes, having lots of people walking up and down and pointing at them," she told him as they hung up their coats in the little staffroom. "If they look at the dogs online, we can bring the ones they want to meet to the visitors' room, so they can get to know them."

Lucy and Adrian and Mattie were busy showing dogs and cats to people hoping to adopt, and whenever they had a spare minute they were working out a plan for a fundraising event at the shopping centre close to Jack's school. So no one noticed that when Jack had finished washing up the dogs' water bowls, he hurried round to Daisy's pen. Her tail was sticking out again, but he was sure the lump under the dog bed looked bigger. She was growing.

"I've got a new book," he explained, waving it at the wire front of the pen. "You probably don't know what sharks are, but they're interesting. They've been around for hundreds of millions of years – I never knew that till I got this book."

He settled down next to the pen and opened up the page about great whites. He started to read, glancing sideways hopefully every so often to see if Daisy was listening.

It took a little while, but by the time Jack was reading about shark attacks – there were only between five and ten attacks on humans every year, which he was surprised about – Daisy had poked her head out from under the bed to listen. When he had read the last of the photo captions on that page, Jack risked looking over at her.

"Hey…" he whispered. The puppy was peering at him, with her nose resting on her paws. When he spoke to her, he was sure he saw the dog bed bounce a little. Was she actually wagging her tail? He didn't want to put her off, so he quickly went back to reading out loud.

When Jack got to the end of the page, Daisy was sitting by the wire, watching him.

"Are you sure?" Amarah asked, looking up at Jack as he leaned over the fence between their gardens.

"Ummm. I think I'm sure. She didn't come out for Mattie or any of the staff at the shelter. I think she likes being read to. We're going over to the shelter in a minute, so you could come and see if she'll do it for you too? Mattie won't mind and Lucy will be OK if we take a note from your mum. We can help Mattie wash up bowls or do something else useful first."

Amarah nodded. "I'll go and see if it's OK." She raced off, but was back in a couple of minutes. "She said yes! Shall I climb over the fence?" Both gardens had benches in just the right place to make it easy to do. "Mum! I'm going now!" She hopped up on to the back of the bench and swung one leg over.

"I'll tell Mattie." Jack dashed into the house.

"Amarah wants to come too?" Mattie stared at him in surprise when he explained. "Why?"

"Because I told her all about Daisy and she wants to see her. We'll both help."

"Um, OK. But you have to be careful," Mattie said, smiling at Amarah as she came in through the back door. "Daisy's so shy, Amarah. We can't scare her. Though actually I noticed she was a bit braver yesterday when I took her dinner in. She looked at me! I know that doesn't sound like much, but it is."

Jack exchanged a hopeful glance with Amarah. It really sounded as if his reading was making Daisy feel better.

At the shelter, Lucy let them help groom two long-haired cats, and play with the black and white kittens that Jack had seen before. After that, though, they managed to hurry round to Daisy's pen before someone could give them another job to do.

The puppy was curled up on her side, but only half tucked under her bed this time – as though she wanted to be close enough to roll back underneath, just in case. She watched cautiously as Jack and Amarah approached her. Then instead of hiding away, she wriggled up on to her paws and came to stand by the wire.

"She never did that before!" Jack whispered.

"You'd better read to her," Amarah breathed. "She almost looks like she's waiting for you to start."

Jack sat on the floor and started to read the page in his book about sawfish. A couple of sentences in, Daisy sat down by the wire front of the pen and yawned.

"She definitely likes it," Amarah whispered and Jack nodded to her. It was almost relaxing, reading with Daisy listening. He'd been a bit worried that Amarah being there would make him feel awkward, but

Amarah was more interested in the dogs than she was in him. When he got to the end of the page, she waved a hand at him. "The others are listening too. Did you know?"

Jack glanced around at the rest of the pens. The dogs *were* all very quiet. Even Pug, who had the pen two down from Daisy, wasn't barking and whining the way he usually did. Jack held the book out to Amarah. "Here," he murmured. "You try. Read some of it to Pug – usually he's yapping all the time."

"OK…" Amarah took the book and sat down in front of Pug's pen. Jack could hear him panting as he came to the wire front to see what was going on. Then he started to bark. Amarah looked anxiously at Jack.

"Am I making him upset?"

"No, he barks a lot, honestly. Read to him. Let's see." Amarah started reading, gabbling nervously over Pug's barks at first, but then slowing down as she began to relax. Pug seemed to relax too. He stopped yapping and then he slumped down to the floor of the pen and started to chew on a rubber bone as he listened.

"It really does work," Jack said, looking around. Pug was chewing. Daisy had gone to lie down, but on top of her bed this time. Bertie, the big ginger Staffie mix, was slumped bonelessly on the floor of his pen, looking half asleep.

Amarah nodded. "They love it."

Chapter Six

"She's got so much better."

Jack nodded, looking down proudly at Daisy. The little white puppy was standing on her hind legs, sniffing Lucy's fingers. It had been two weeks since Jack had first seen her, and Daisy hardly ever hid under her basket now – only when there was a lot of barking from the other dogs.

Lucy had let him go into the pen
with Daisy a few times – after they'd
checked with Mum –
and it was a real treat,
getting to stroke her
and fuss over her.
Her white fur
looked as if
it would be
wiry, but
she was
incredibly
soft, and her
peachy ears were like warm velvet. Jack
couldn't help imagining sitting on the
sofa at home with her, stroking those
ears while they watched TV.

"You wouldn't think she was the
same dog," Mattie said, crouching

down to let Daisy sniff her hands too, and Daisy wagged her tail wildly.

"She's still got a way to go, but she's getting really friendly." Lucy smiled at Jack. "Who knew reading to a dog could make such a difference!"

Jack beamed back at her. Since he'd discovered the secret – it still felt like a secret, an amazing discovery – he had been going back to the shelter with Mattie as often as he could. He could visit for a short while after school most weekdays and he got to be there for longer at the weekends. Since it was a Sunday, he'd been helping Lucy all afternoon, and she'd let him take some of the dogs into the little yard so he could throw toys for them to chase. It seemed like a lot of fun to Jack, but

Lucy promised it was really useful.

Jack did most of his reading with Daisy, but sometimes he read to the other dogs too. Pug was definitely less yappy after Jack had sat with him for a while – and it was helping Jack's reading too. Mr Gardner had told Mum that there had been *a definite improvement*.

Jack had even been doing extra reading online, trying to find out more ways to help Daisy. He and Amarah had found a shelter website that showed how to make a special treat mat, to keep bored dogs busy. Mattie had let him have the scruffy old fleece with holes in that she used to wear at the shelter. Mum had given her a new one for her birthday and Mattie had only been going to throw the old one away. He and Amarah had spent ages cutting up strips of fabric – Amarah's mum had given them one of Anika's polo shirts that was covered in whiteboard pen as well.

They'd tied the strips through the holes in the square of fleece, so it looked like a sort of fluffy doormat. Jack had finished it the night before and brought it with him to try out with Daisy when it was time for her dinner. If she liked it, he was thinking he could make some more, maybe one for every dog at the shelter.

"I'm going to help get your dinner ready now," he told Daisy after Lucy and Mattie had gone. He was kneeling on the floor outside her pen, so her nose was on a level with his if she stood on her back legs. He giggled as she swiped her tongue through the wire and licked him, and he had to wipe dog slobber off his cheek. "Uuurgh. I love you too. Back in a bit, OK?"

In the kitchen, Jack helped Mattie measure out the food, and then he took a handful of biscuits from Daisy's bowl and hid them one by one inside the fluffy mat. It was supposed to make eating more fun as the dogs snuffled out the food. It looked good, he thought, eyeing it proudly.

"You didn't say you'd finished it!" Mattie said, coming back in to grab more food bowls. "Are you going to try it out?"

"Yeah! Want to come and see?"

They headed back to Daisy's pen and Jack put her usual food bowl down first. He had a feeling that if she was really hungry, the treat mat might not be as much fun. If *he* was starving, having to search for his dinner would definitely make him grumpy. Then he left the mat in the corner of the pen and he and Mattie stood outside to watch.

Daisy wolfed down her food in about a minute, like she usually did, but she could clearly smell that there was more around somewhere. She sniffed her way over to the mat and started to root around in it eagerly, nosing out each biscuit and crunching it up. Jack could tell she really liked it – her tail was wagging excitedly and her ears were pricked right up.

"That's a hit," Mattie whispered.
"Wow, I thought it would take her
longer. She must have found nearly all
the food."

Daisy was slowing down now. She
nibbled one more treat out of the mat
and then slumped down next to it.
It looked as if she was trying to hold
the mat in her paws and cuddle it and
Mattie put her hand over her mouth to
stop herself laughing.

"She's going underneath it! Look!"
Jack nudged his sister and they

watched as Daisy snuffled her way under the treat mat, so that she was a little white dog with a fluffy blue head. "I think she's falling asleep. She still likes sleeping with something over her head, doesn't she?"

"Maybe she always will," Mattie said a little sadly. "I suppose dogs remember things they learn when they're little. It's a habit for her now." Then she put her arm round Jack and hugged him. "Sorry! I didn't mean to bring you down. She's always going to remember you reading to her as well, you know." Then she looked at her watch and made a face. "I'd better get on with feeding everyone now."

Jack crouched down, watching Daisy breathing gently as she slept. She was still so small, the mat could have covered her completely.

"Hey…" someone whispered next to him.

"Mum!" Jack jumped up. "I didn't even see you."

"I know! Sorry, I didn't mean to scare you. Time to head back home."

"Do we have to?" Jack sighed.

"Yes, it's nearly your dinner time as well!" Mum smiled at him. "I'm really impressed, you know. You've been spending so much time helping out here."

"I like it. I love dogs – I didn't know how much till I started coming here with Mattie."

Mum nodded. "I can see that." She took a deep breath. "Look, Jack, I've been thinking – would you like us to get a dog of our own?"

Jack stopped watching Daisy's soft, sleepy breathing and turned to stare at his mum. Did she mean it? They could have a dog? They could have Daisy?

He'd never even let himself hope that he could take her home. Earlier on, when Lucy had said how much better she was, he'd been so pleased. And then a little voice in his head had pointed out, *That means somebody could adopt her soon. Someone's going to take Daisy away. They might even change her name, and she wouldn't be your Daisy any more.* He'd squashed the voice down, and then Lucy had said she still had a way to go and the relief had just surged through him. *Not yet!*

"Yes!" he yelped and Daisy twitched under the treat mat. She wriggled and then her whiskery muzzle appeared and her dark eyes shone up at him from under the fluffy fabric. "I mean, yes, that would be amazing," he added in a quieter voice, grinning at Daisy. "She's—"

"I always thought it would be too difficult to cope with, but helping with the dogs here seems to have been so good for you. Of course, we'd have to make sure it was the right dog," Mum went on and Jack nodded. That made sense. Daisy was absolutely the right dog.

"Probably an older dog that's really calm? I expect Lucy could help us choose one."

Jack went on nodding for a second or two until he actually heard what Mum had said. *An older dog. Calm.*

"It wouldn't be good to have a puppy. We haven't got time to do a lot of training, when we're all so busy. But I could pop home from work at lunchtime to do a quick walk, and maybe Mattie could too sometimes."

Jack kept his eyes fixed on Daisy. He'd been so excited, so happy, for all of half a minute. How could only thirty seconds of hoping make everything seem so much worse now? It was as if he'd been given the most amazing present and then had it snatched away from him again. In fact, that was exactly what had happened.

From underneath the raggedy mat, Daisy watched Jack walk away, her ears drooping. He was going! He never went without saying goodbye to her. Even if he was on the other side of the wire, he always rubbed her ears and told her how beautiful she was.

She scrambled up, whining, but he didn't turn and run back. It was as if he couldn't even hear her. She whined louder, scrabbling her claws against the wire door, and then she gave a sharp little bark – but Jack disappeared round the corner of the passage without even looking back.

She stared out for a moment or two, her nose jammed in the gap between the wires. Then she turned away and picked up the treat mat in her teeth. It smelled of Jack – Jack and biscuits. Daisy took the mat with her as she crawled underneath her bed.

Chapter Seven

"What's the matter with you?" Amarah hissed as Mr Gardner turned away.

Jack just shrugged.

"You knew how to do that sum, easy! Why didn't you do it?"

"Just leave me alone!" Jack stretched his legs out under the table and kicked Aaron's chair leg. And again. And then again.

"Oi! Stop it!" Aaron muttered. "I can tell it's you, Jack."

"Mr Gardner's watching you," Lily said in a sing-song voice. "You'll get into trouble!" She sounded quite excited about it.

Jack stopped kicking Aaron's chair and wrapped his feet round the legs of his own chair instead. He felt like he needed to glue himself down. It had been the same ever since yesterday. Mum and Mattie kept talking about dogs at the shelter, and which ones would make good pets. They both seemed really excited about it. Mum was even thinking about adopting Pug.

All he wanted to do was yell, *No! It has to be Daisy! I only want Daisy!* How could they even think he'd ever be happy with a different dog?

He made a strange noise, a sort of choking, gasping noise, and Amarah looked at him sharply. "Are you going to be sick?"

Jack shook his head, but he wasn't actually sure. He felt awful.

"Here." Amarah handed him her water bottle and he gulped from it gratefully. He wasn't going to be sick, it was just that he really, really wanted to cry, he realized. But he couldn't, not here, not in front of everybody.

"Is something wrong with Daisy?" Amarah whispered and Jack stared at her.

"How did you know?"

Amarah shrugged. "Hunch. You've been so much better at school since you started helping at the shelter and spending all that time with her. Now you've gone back to being weird and moody again."

"Who's Daisy?" Lily leaned over to ask. "Oooooh! Has Jack got a *girlfriend*?"

Amarah scowled at her. "Grow up," she snapped. "What are you, five?" and Lily went scarlet.

Jack put his hand over his mouth to stop himself laughing out loud. "Thanks," he muttered to Amarah. "My mum said we could adopt a dog."

Amarah shook her head. "I don't

get it! That's fantastic! Why are you upset?" Then she stared down at her maths like it was the most interesting thing she'd ever seen. "Mr Gardner's glaring at us," she said out the side of her mouth. "Tell me at break, OK?"

At break time, Amarah dragged Jack over to one of the benches and handed him half her banana. "I don't understand. I thought you really wanted a dog!"

Jack shook his head gloomily and squished the end of the banana between his fingers. He couldn't face eating it. "Nope. I want Daisy."

"So why can't you adopt her? Is she still too little? You could wait a bit, though, couldn't you?"

"It isn't that. Mum says we need to get an older dog that's calm. You know, well behaved. No puppies, because they're too hyper."

"What, so your mum doesn't want a dog version of you?" Amarah gave a snort.

Jack sighed. "Yeah."

"Sorry." Amarah's face fell. "That was meant to be a joke."

"It's true, though."

"But you've been loads better,"

Amarah pointed out. "Mr Gardner told your mum how good you've been. I heard him. That's all because of Daisy. Doesn't your mum understand that? Why didn't you tell her?"

"I don't know! I didn't think she'd listen. She said not a puppy." Jack handed the banana back to Amarah and wrapped his arms tightly round his middle, as if he was giving himself a hug.

"Yes, but Daisy's not just *any* puppy, is she?" Amarah shook her head. "You have to tell her. Didn't your sister say anything? Mattie knows how special Daisy is."

"Yeah…" Jack leaned back against the bench. "Maybe Mum would listen to Mattie," he admitted.

"Mattie, and me, and you," Amarah said firmly. "Your sister's taking you to the shelter again this afternoon, isn't she? So you have to explain everything to her. You can both tell your mum later, and I'll come round and tell her too."

Jack nodded slowly. Maybe Amarah was right – he *hadn't* told Mum how he felt about Daisy, he'd just expected her to know. He had to speak up.

Daisy's nose was just peeping out from under her bed, but she'd pulled the bed up close to the wire door so she could see what was happening. She was watching for Jack. Every time anyone had walked down the passage that day, she'd wriggled out a little more to see who it was. But it was never him. Daisy knew that usually Jack came later on, but still she couldn't help hoping. She was starting to feel hungry for dinner now, and he often arrived just before dinner time. Soon…

There was a scuffling, and footsteps, and Daisy scooted out from under the bed to look down the passage. There was a boy… Her ears pricked up hopefully.

No, not Jack yet. It was Lucy with a group of people Daisy didn't know.

"We do have one lovely young puppy actually, but she's a little nervous. I'm not sure she's ready for a busy family home just yet."

The group moved off towards the main reception area and Daisy slumped down on the floor again. When was he going to come?

Then her tail hunched between her legs and a shudder ran over her. What if he didn't come back? What if he'd left her, like the people who'd thrown her out of the car? Daisy was almost sure that Jack was hers. But they had been her people too.

She whimpered and scuffled the blue treat mat under her paws to catch the smell of food, and Jack, and home.

Jack ran down the passage to the corner where Daisy's pen was. He had a strange feeling in his stomach, as if she might have disappeared. All afternoon he'd been daydreaming – whenever Mr Gardner wasn't watching, anyway – thinking about what would happen after he'd explained to Mum. He *had* to make her understand. Amarah was right.

He'd imagined him and Daisy running round the park. Or Daisy asleep on his lap while he was doing his homework or watching TV. Maybe even asleep on the end of his bed. It all felt so real, it was too good to be true…

No, there she was, scrabbling wildly

at the side of her pen. She was so excited she was actually squeaking.

"Did you miss me?" Jack asked her, laughing. He caught her paws through the wire pen, hot little paws with hard black nails. "I missed you. Let me look at you…" It felt as if he was looking at her properly for the first time, now that there was a chance, just a chance, that she might be his dog.

She was so beautiful, even when she was jumping up and down and then darting off to whirl round her pen and flinging herself back to lick frantically at his fingers.

"Shhhh, shhh…" Jack said gently. "It's OK, Daisy. It's OK."

There were footsteps at the other end of the passage and he saw Lucy walking towards him with Mattie behind her. Lucy had a clipboard and a pen – she was tapping the pen against her teeth as if she was thinking.

"Hello! How's she doing, Jack?"

"Good. She was a bit excited, but she's calming down now." Jack looked back at Daisy, who was standing close to the wire, looking uncertain.

"I was just talking to a family who are looking for a puppy," Lucy explained. "Or a young dog anyway." She sighed. "I did try to suggest one of our lovely old-age pensioners, but they wanted a dog who'd be really active. Anyway –" she smiled at Jack – "I wondered about Daisy. What do you both think?" She looked round at Mattie. "You've done so much work

socializing her, especially you, Jack.
Do you think she'd cope with a family?
It's actually only one boy and he's ten,
so not too young."

Mattie nodded eagerly. "I think
they'd have to take things slow, but
yes. Daisy's such a gorgeous dog, she
deserves a lovely home."

"No!" Jack yelped, and Daisy gave a worried whine and scraped one front paw against the concrete.

Mattie frowned at him. "Hey, gently."

"Sorry." Jack swallowed hard. He had to get this right. He had to make Lucy and Mattie understand – he'd meant to talk to Mum first, but he couldn't let Lucy give Daisy to somebody else. Not *his* dog. He crouched down and let Daisy snuffle at his fingers while he tried to think what to say.

"Did Mattie tell you that our mum said we could adopt a dog?" he asked Lucy.

She nodded, smiling. "Yes, it's brilliant news. I know Mattie's been desperate to have one for a while, and you're just such a dog person, Jack."

Jack tried to smile back, but his face felt stiff. "Maybe. I'm not sure if I'm really a dog person. It's … I mean … I only want Daisy!"

"Oh…" Mattie started to shake her head. "But Mum said…"

"I know," Jack broke in quickly. "We have to have a sensible dog. One of the old-age pensioners." He nodded at Lucy. "But Mum's saying that because I'm…" He faltered. "Um. Sometimes I'm not very sensible. Except I am. I could be. If it was Daisy. All that reading to her – I worked really hard – and she's so much better. We're *good* for each other."

Lucy beamed at him and reached down to pat his shoulder. "I know you are. You've been amazing with her and you can tell she's bonded with you." She glanced back at Mattie. "That was actually something I was a bit worried about – whether Daisy would ever build up such a good relationship with her new owner. But I couldn't stop Jack helping her, not when it was making such a difference."

Jack nodded eagerly. "Could you –
please could you tell my mum that?
That we don't need a sensible old dog?"
He looked hopefully at Mattie. "You
like her too, don't you?"

Mattie crouched down and looked
at the little white face peering back
at them anxiously through the wire.
"Silly question," she said lovingly, and
laughed as Daisy dabbed a cold black
nose against her hand. "OK. Now
we've just got to convince Mum."

Chapter Eight

"I'm not at all sure about this." Jack's mum sighed. "A puppy! And a puppy who's had a hard time and isn't very reliable! That's exactly what I said I *didn't* want."

Mattie had called her mum and asked her to come by the shelter on her way home from work. Now Mum and Lucy and Mattie and Jack were all sitting in the visitors' room with Daisy. Jack had Daisy on his lap and she was half asleep, curled snugly against his school jumper. It was already covered in white hairs, but he didn't mind. He'd get them off with sticky tape if Mum was worried, but he loved it that Daisy had left a mark on him. It felt like he belonged to her.

Lucy nodded seriously. "I know exactly what you mean. But actually she's settling down amazingly well. She was very young when we got her, and yes she'd been abandoned and she was very withdrawn and nervous, but that's changed over the last few weeks. And I have to tell you, that's mostly down to Jack." She smiled at him and Jack grinned back at her shyly. He still wasn't used to people saying such nice things about him. "He's worked so hard. He's too young to be an official volunteer at the shelter like Mattie, but I'm really hoping he'll keep coming to help. Even when you have your own dog at home, Jack."

Jack nodded eagerly. "My friend Amarah wants to keep coming here as well," he told Lucy. "We wondered – do you think you could make it an official thing, us reading to the dogs? They all like it. And we thought maybe we could send a message to the schools around here, asking for more volunteers. So that there's someone reading to the dogs after school every day. Or some schools might walk children round to the shelter in their lunch break."

"Wow." Lucy blinked, looking surprised. "We could definitely think about it."

"It would mean more people coming to the shelter," Mattie pointed out. "We're always trying to think of ways to get more people in to see the dogs and cats."

Jack nodded. There were so many dogs who'd been at the shelter for a long time – they were desperate for proper homes. He ran one of Daisy's soft ears through his fingers and she snuffled sleepily.

"It would help with the children's reading as well," he added. "Schools would like that. I got loads better, just from reading out loud to Daisy and the others."

Lucy and Mum were nodding as if they agreed and Jack ducked his head to hide his proud grin. He was persuading them!

"That all sounds great," Jack's mum said slowly, "but I'm still worried about us adopting Daisy. How are we going to cope with a puppy?"

"It's tricky," Lucy admitted. "We usually say that someone needs to be home most of the time, to make sure young dogs aren't lonely."

"I can pop home from college if I have a free period," Mattie pointed out. "Most days I do. And you said you could come home at lunchtime, Mum. She'd get lots of little walks. Jack and I could take her out for a proper run before school."

"Amarah asked her mum this afternoon," Jack said eagerly. "She said she doesn't mind coming round to check on Daisy sometimes too. Daisy's so good, Mum, just look at her." He edged closer to his mum on the sofa and the puppy opened one eye lazily and yawned. "You could stroke her?" he suggested.

Mum reached out one hand and ran it gently down Daisy's back. "She's very soft," she told Jack, smiling. "Hello, sweetheart…" she added as Daisy wriggled round and licked the back of her hand. "You are very cute, aren't you? And I can see how much she loves you both. Maybe it would be all right." Then she gave a surprised laugh as Daisy wobbled upright and

stomped over on
to her lap instead.
The little white
dog slumped
down again with
a massive yawn
and seemed to go
back to sleep. "Oh …
I wasn't expecting that."
Mum rubbed Daisy's ears, and
looked up at Jack and Mattie. "I think
she might have decided for us…"

Daisy wriggled a little in Jack's arms,
turning so she could gaze up at him.
He looked afraid and she could smell
the worry rising off him. She pressed

her nose gently into the gap under his chin and felt him catch his breath in a half laugh. "Thanks," he whispered, rubbing his cheek against the top of her head. "This is really scary."

Daisy felt him step forward and then Amarah held up a piece of paper in front of her nose. Daisy leaned out of Jack's arms to sniff it and then she nibbled the bottom corner. The crowd of people in front of them laughed and Daisy beat her tail against Jack's arm. She didn't know what was happening, but she liked the noise. Jack started to read out loud.

"Thank you for coming to the fundraiser for Tall Pines Animal Shelter. Today we are launching a new scheme to help animals, and children…"

Daisy sighed happily, resting her nose on his shoulder.

"I started to read to my dog Daisy when she was still at Tall Pines, after being abandoned. I didn't know the amazing effect reading to dogs could have. Please help us…"

"You did so well!" Mattie hugged Jack, trying not to squash Daisy, and Daisy squirmed delightedly. "I could hear people in the crowd saying how gorgeous Daisy is."

"I can't believe I read in front of all those people," Jack murmured. He was still feeling a bit shaky.

"I can't believe you did either. You were brilliant." Mattie stroked Daisy's nose. "And so were you, little one."

"Lucy says lots of people are asking about making appointments to visit," Amarah told them excitedly, pointing at the board behind Jack, which was plastered with big photos of the dogs at the shelter. "Someone wants to come and see Pug! She said she's always had pugs and he's really beautiful!"

"I'd better go and help write down some details," Mattie said, darting away, and Jack sat down on the edge of the little platform. Daisy wriggled out of his arms and started to sniff around their feet. The shopping centre was full of intriguing smells.

"How are you doing?" Amarah asked, sitting next to him. "I was a bit worried you might run away just before it was your speech."

"Me too." Jack shivered. "But it was OK. It sounded like I was talking to the crowd, but actually I just read it to Daisy."

Daisy heard her name and looked round. Then she jumped up next to him again, squishing in between Jack and Amarah and nosing lovingly at both of them. She sank down with her muzzle on Jack's knee and gazed up at him with huge dark eyes.

"Do you want to go home?" Jack whispered to her. "Me too. It's OK, Daisy, we'll be home soon, I promise."

Daisy thumped her tail lazily against Amarah's legs and then wriggled further up so she was slumped half on to Jack's lap. She didn't mind where they went, as long as Jack came with her.

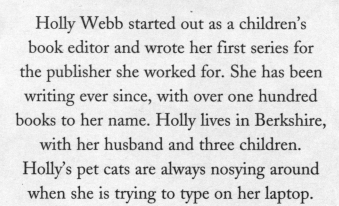

HOLLY WEBB

Holly Webb started out as a children's
book editor and wrote her first series for
the publisher she worked for. She has been
writing ever since, with over one hundred
books to her name. Holly lives in Berkshire,
with her husband and three children.
Holly's pet cats are always nosying around
when she is trying to type on her laptop.

For more information
about Holly Webb visit:

www.holly-webb.com